Vera Jewel

is Late for School

honk honk

Nicola Kent

MACMILLAN CHILDREN'S BOOKS

On Monday morning, Vera Jewel
Hopped on her bike to ride to school.

But a great big spike,

Meant a broken bike.

And Vera Jewel . . .

. . . was late for school.

Vera Jewel felt quite forlorn.
She loved that bike, those wheels, that horn!
Scratched her head . . . what instead?

Skateboard?

Scooter?

Unicorn?

Tuesday morning, Vera Jewel

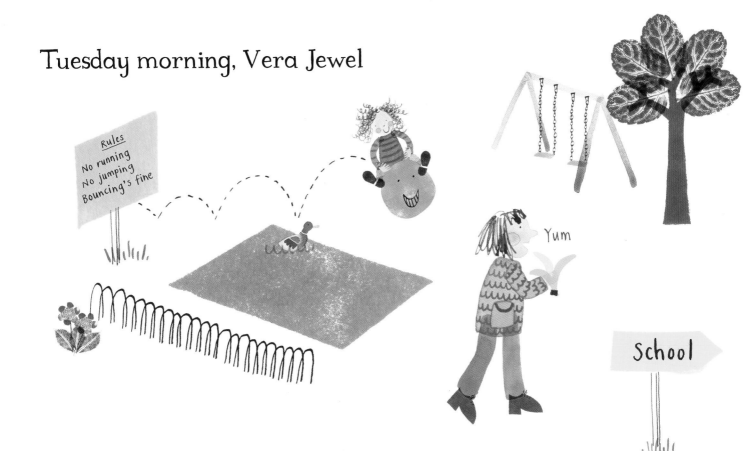

Was bouncing past the paddling pool.

Banana skin . . .

And Vera Jewel . . .

Squeeze

. . . was late for school.

Sorry Sir

Vera!

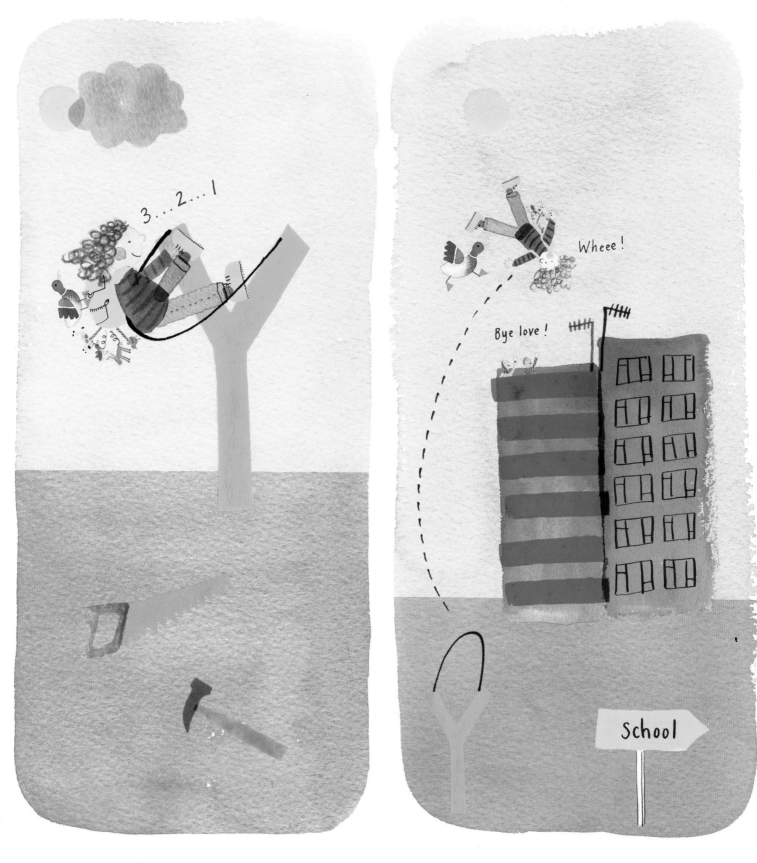

Wednesday morning,
Vera Jewel

Built a special travel tool.

But what a pain . . .   She's home again!

And Vera Jewel was late for school.

Vera! It's nearly lunchtime!

Sorry sir!

Jangle

Toot

Ting

Thursday morning, Vera Jewel
Bought her neighbour's champion mule.

Off they dashed . . .

Sorry Sir

VERA!
Are you ok?

And Vera Jewel
was late for school.

Friday morning, Vera Jewel
Filled a plane with rocket fuel.

Vera soon . . .

Bye love!

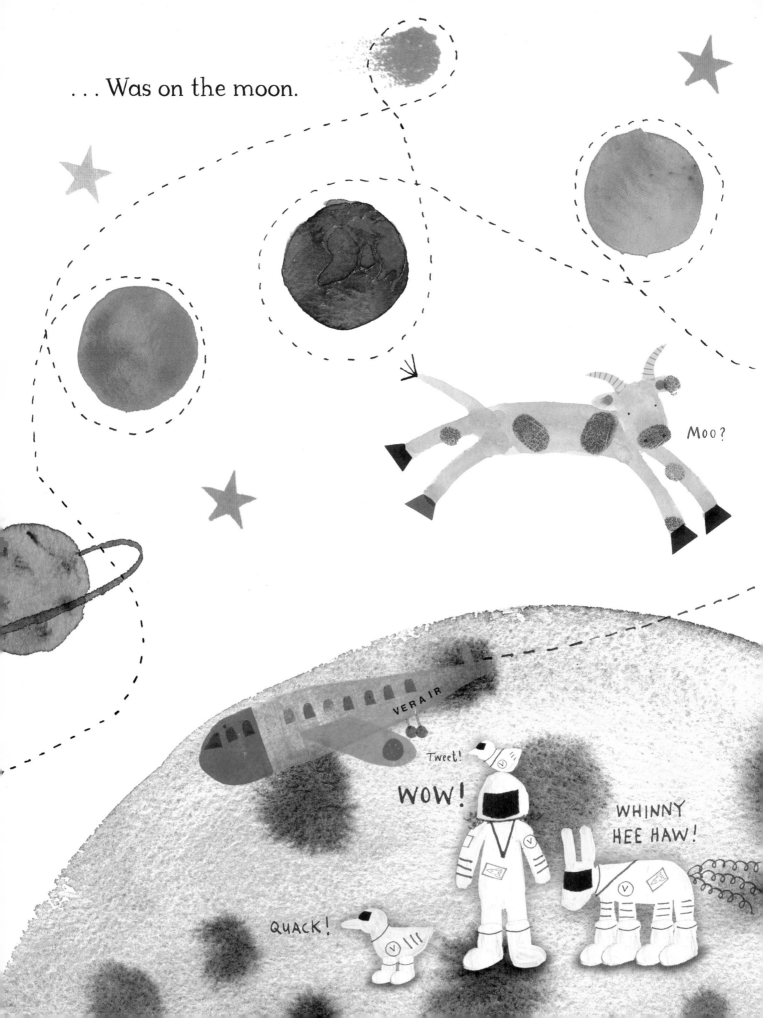

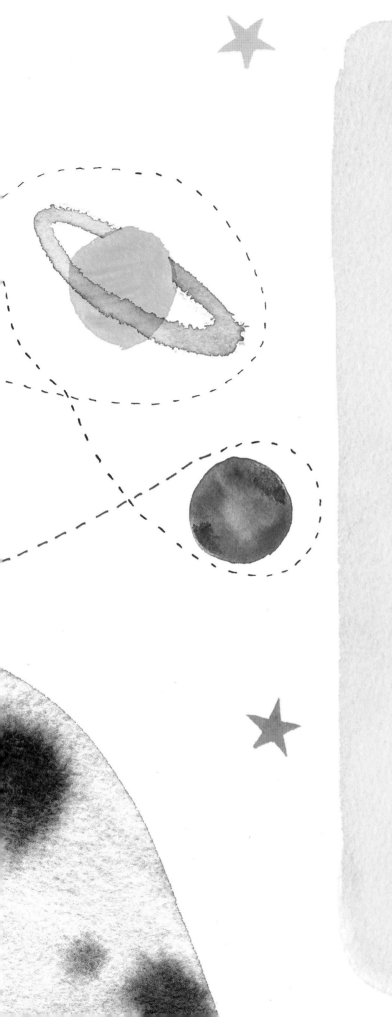

And Vera Jewel
was late for school.

Sorry sir

Vera!
Home time was half an hour ago!

Friday night and Vera Jewel

Camped outside the door
to school.

She woke on time,   Was first in line . . .

Now Vera's feeling really blue.
It seems there's nothing left to do!
Why did that spike
Have to break her bike?

But wait . . .

. . . Eureka! She's got it! Phew!

100% Organic mega-nourishing mobile meadow for jumping cows at rest

Recycled travel tool handlebars for accurate steering

Super-comfy ultra-padded bottom-friendly seat

120 miles per hour running machine for champion mules in training

Moon rock-armoured spike-proof speedy wheels for punctual girls

VERAIR

Plane tail for extra whoosh

Pure pond water with no artificial additives for ducks in transit

Helmet with built-in luxury fleece-lined nest for birds a-laying

All through Sunday and half the night,
Vera works to fix her plight.

And Monday morning, what a surprise!
Her teacher can't believe his eyes.

Wow Vera!

Morning Sir!

It's Vera Jewel . . .
ON TIME FOR SCHOOL!
And her special bike is . . .

SUPERSIZE!

It's super fast, it's super cool,
This bicycle's the talk of school.
And when class ends, now all her friends
Love riding home with Vera Jewel!

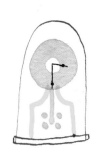

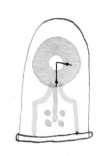